Dear Parent:
Your child's love of reading starts here!

Every child learns to read in a different way and at his or her own speed. Some go back and forth between reading levels and read favorite books again and again. Others read through each level in order. You can help your young reader improve and become more confident by encouraging his or her own interests and abilities. From books your child reads with you to the first books he or she reads alone, there are I Can Read Books for every stage of reading:

SHARED READING
Basic language, word repetition, and whimsical illustrations, ideal for sharing with your emergent reader

BEGINNING READING
Short sentences, familiar words, and simple concepts for children eager to read on their own

READING WITH HELP
Engaging stories, longer sentences, and language play for developing readers

READING ALONE
Complex plots, challenging vocabulary, and high-interest topics for the independent reader

ADVANCED READING
Short paragraphs, chapters, and exciting themes for the perfect bridge to chapter books

I Can Read Books have introduced children to the joy of reading since 1957. Featuring award-winning authors and illustrators and a fabulous cast of beloved characters, I Can Read Books set the standard for beginning readers.

A lifetime of discovery begins with the magical words "I Can Read!"

Visit www.icanread.com for information
on enriching your child's reading experience.

For Renee B.
—D.C.

For Ruby Nichols
—H.B.

I Can Read Book® is a trademark of HarperCollins Publishers.

Diary of a Worm: Nat the Gnat
Text copyright © 2014 by Doreen Cronin
Illustrations copyright © 2014 by Harry Bliss
All rights reserved. Printed in the United States of America.
No part of this book may be used or reproduced in any manner whatsoever without written permission except in the case of brief quotations embodied in critical articles and reviews. For information address HarperCollins Children's Books, a division of HarperCollins Publishers, 195 Broadway, New York, NY 10007.
www.icanread.com

Library of Congress catalog card number: 2013950294
ISBN 978-0-06-208708-9 (trade bdg.)—ISBN 978-0-06-208707-2 (pbk.)

15   16   17   PC/WOR   10 9 8 7 6 5 4 3   ❖   First Edition

I Can Read!

BEGINNING 1 READING

DIARY OF A WORM

Nat the Gnat

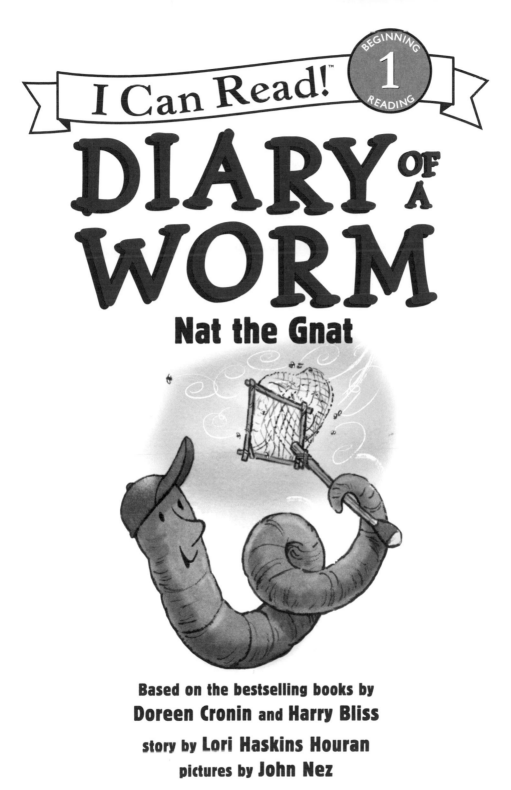

Based on the bestselling books by
Doreen Cronin and **Harry Bliss**

story by **Lori Haskins Houran**
pictures by **John Nez**

HARPER
An Imprint of HarperCollinsPublishers

January 10

My class got a pet today!

I told Spider about him after school.

"Our gnat is so cute," I said.

"We just have to name him."

"Didn't you say his name?"
asked Spider. "You said Nat."
"No," I said. "Not Nat. *Gnat.*"
"Nat Nat?" said Spider.

7

It was a confusing talk.

But it did help me come up with the perfect name for our pet.

January 11

Mrs. Mulch taught our class
all about gnats.

Gnat Facts
1. They love wet stuff,
   just like worms do.

2. They're tiny, even when
   they're grown up.

3. They fly around at
   dusk in swarms
   called ghosts.

Then Mrs. Mulch said we'll take turns caring for Nat.

Gnat Facts
1. They love wet stuff, just like worms do.

2. They're tiny, even when they're grown up.

3. They fly around at dusk in swarms called ghosts.

My day is tomorrow.

I can't wait.

It's going to be the best day ever!

January 12

Today is the worst day ever.

I LOST OUR CLASS PET!

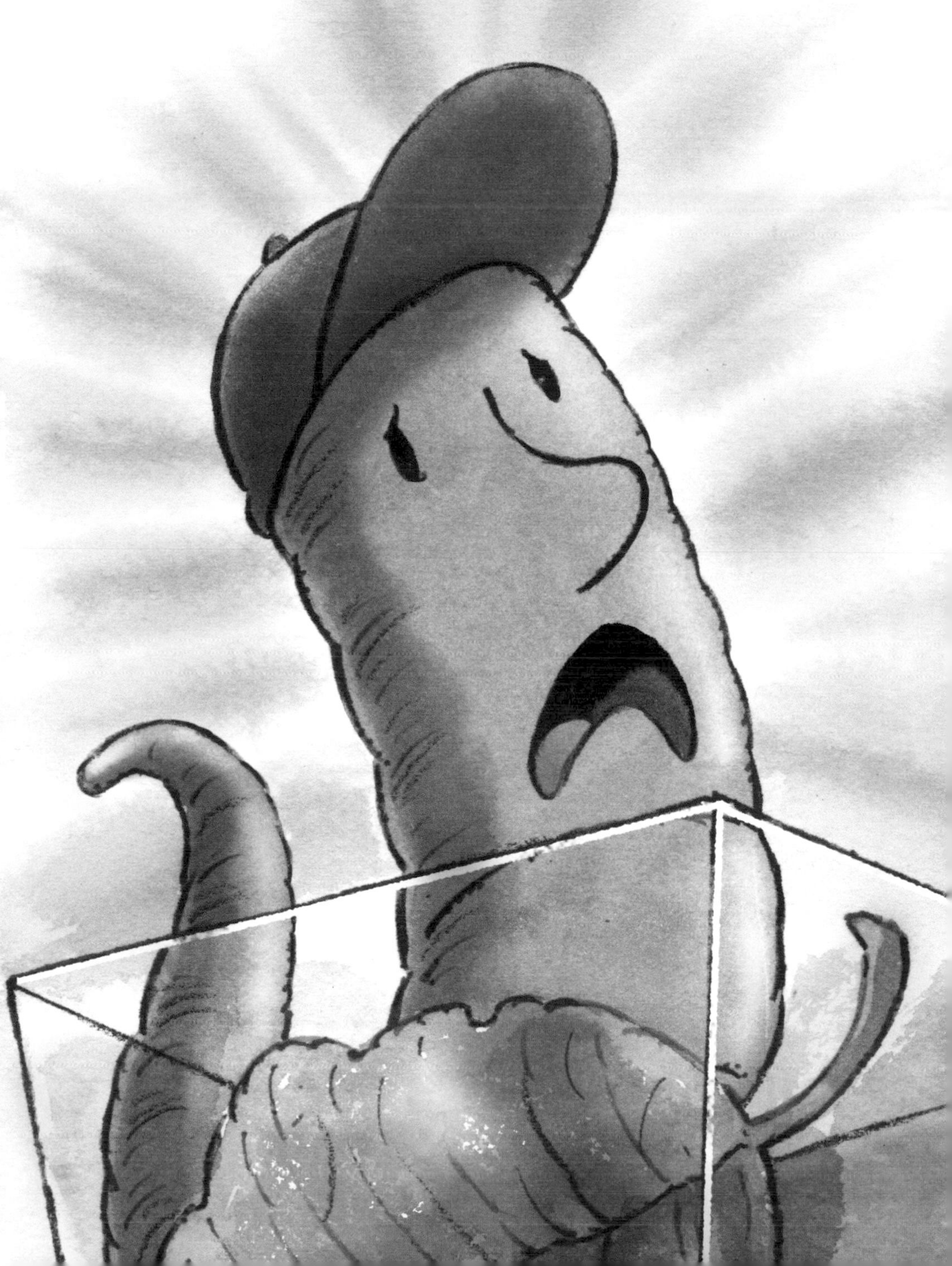

Here's what happened:

This morning, I brought Nat

a nice wet leaf.

I opened his tank to put in the leaf.

Then I closed it and went out

for recess.

At least, I thought I'd closed it.

But when I got back, Nat was GONE!

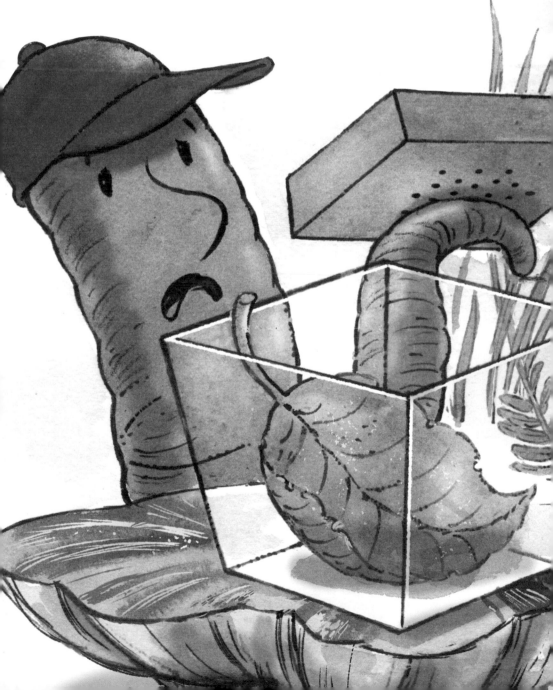

The whole rest of the day,

I argued with myself.

Tell Mrs. Mulch!

Don't tell her!

Tell her!

Don't tell her!

Guess which side won?

January 13

I went over to Spider's last night.

I had to tell someone my secret.

"What am I going to do?" I said.

"I'm in big trouble on Monday."

Suddenly I saw something
in the air.

"Look!" I whispered. "A ghost!"

"A GHOST?!" yelled Spider.

The ghost of gnats gave

me an idea.

"Spider, what if I took

one of those gnats to school?

Just until I found the real Nat."

Then I stopped myself.

"That's impossible," I said.

"How would I ever catch a gnat?"

Spider looked at me and smiled.
"Gee, too bad you don't have
any friends who can spin webs."

Spider helped me make

a gnat trap.

After a few tries, I got a gnat.

This idea just might work!

January 15

I did it.

I put the gnat in Nat's tank

this morning.

No one could tell.

No one but me.

I felt horrible.

All of a sudden I stood up.

"That gnat's not Nat!" I said.

"I lost him and I put
a different gnat in his tank!"

Mrs. Mulch gasped.

A bunch of kids rushed over

to look in the tank.

"Hey!" said one of the kids.

"There are TWO gnats in there!

One just flew out

from under a leaf!"

I couldn't believe it.

Nat had been there all along,

right under the leaf I'd given him!

Mrs. Mulch forgave me.
"It was brave of you
to tell the truth," she said.

The class forgave me, too.
After all, now we have
two class pets . . .

Nat and Pat!